THE
Bootlegger's
GODDAUGHTER

THE
Bootlegger's
GODDAUGHTER

MELODIE CAMPBELL

RAVEN BOOKS
an imprint of
ORCA BOOK PUBLISHERS

Library and Archives Canada Cataloguing in Publication

Campbell, Melodie, 1955–, author
The bootlegger's goddaughter / Melodie Campbell.
(Rapid Reads)

Issued also in print and electronic formats.
ISBN 978-1-4598-1413-4 (pbk.).—ISBN 978-1-4598-1414-1 (pdf).—
ISBN 978-1-4598-1415-8 (epub)

I. Title. II. Series: Rapid reads
PS8605.A54745B66 2017   C813'.6   C2016-904470-X
C2016-904471-8

First published in the United States, 2017
Library of Congress Control Number: 2016950243

Summary: In this work of crime fiction, Gina works to uncover a bootlegging
operation that threatens to jeopardize her wedding. (RL 3.0)

*Orca Book Publishers is dedicated to preserving the environment and has
printed this book on Forest Stewardship Council® certified paper.*

Orca Book Publishers gratefully acknowledges the support for
its publishing programs provided by the following agencies:
the Government of Canada through the Canada Book Fund and the
Canada Council for the Arts, and the Province of British Columbia
through the BC Arts Council and the Book Publishing Tax Credit.

Cover design by Jenn Playford
Cover photography by iStock.com

ORCA BOOK PUBLISHERS
www.orcabook.com

Printed and bound in Canada.

20 19 18 17 • 4 3 2 1

For Alison and her crow.

ONE

My cell phone rang, and it was Nico.

"Where are you?" he said. His tenor voice was a tad strident.

"At the corner of King and James. Hold on a sec while I put something down."

I was carrying too much, as usual. My arms ached from the weight. I placed the reusable shopping bag I'd been carrying on the sidewalk. Then I tucked my small handbag into the top of it. I leaned back against a storefront window with the phone to my ear, drinking in the winter sun that shone down on my face.

It was a beautiful December day in Hamilton, also known as The Hammer. You could hardly smell the smog from the steel plants in the distance. The temperature was just above freezing, with no snow in the forecast. Santa might have a bit of trouble with that, but I was happy. My wedding was in three days. I didn't need crappy weather or anything else to mess with it.

"What's up?" I asked my favorite cousin. Nico is a few years younger than me. He owns the interior-design store next door to my jewelry shop.

"Have you heard about the storm?" he said.

"What storm?" I looked up into the sky. It was bright blue, and the sun was big and shiny.

"Not here," said Nico. "Starting late tomorrow, hitting the eastern seaboard."

I hadn't noticed the skinny young guy until he was right at my side. "Lady, you got a light?" he said.

My attention slipped from the phone call to his unshaven face. He was wearing dirty jeans and a ragged black band T-shirt. He seemed vaguely familiar. "Sorry, I don't—hey!"

Quick as a weasel, the creep grabbed my shopping bag. He turned and ran.

"Stop!" I yelled. I took off after him, phone still in my hand.

"Gina, what's happening?" Nico's voice sounded far, far away.

The kid ran fast, whipping around the other walkers on James Street. I followed as quickly as I could in dress boots, which wasn't fast enough. *Why the hell did I wear heels today?*

Down James we both ran, weaving between startled pedestrians. I saw him tangle with a homeless man, spinning him around. I dodged an old lady with a trundle cart and smacked into a younger one pushing an umbrella stroller.

"Sorry," I said, untangling myself from her arm. "Sorry."

The race continued. I ran past the homeless man, clipping him with my elbow. "Sorry," I sang out.

The light turned red in front of us, but my quarry ignored it. He sprinted through the intersection without slowing down. I cursed, slowed and looked left and right for cars before picking up the chase.

My wraparound coat was wide open now, flowing like a cape behind me. I felt it catch on something, then release. "Oops, sorry," I mumbled to a lamppost.

My target swung around a corner and onto a side street. I peeled around the corner after him. He dashed across the street and looked back.

"Hey!" I yelled again, from my side of the road.

I could almost see him smile. I leapt out into the street, determined not to lose him.

Honk!

"Sorry," I mumbled to the car that had missed me by inches.

"Watch where you're going, moron!" yelled the driver of the car.

I patted the lid of the trunk with my left hand as I ran by.

In retrospect, it probably sounded like a smack.

By this time, the skinny kid was way ahead of me. I vaulted up onto the sidewalk, caught my heel on the curb and lost my balance. *Damn!* By the time I got upright, he was crossing John Street. No way could I catch up.

I doubled over, hands on knees for balance, gasping for air.

He stopped for a moment to look back. Then he raised his arm and waved.

"That's not fair!" I yelled after the fleeing figure. "I'm supposed to be the thief around here, dammit."

TWO

I was a tad miffed when Nico picked me up in his little red Beetle half an hour later.

"What did he steal?" said Nico.

"Everything," I said, sliding into the passenger seat. "My wallet, credit cards, Christmas presents. Even my car keys. *Shit.*" I slammed the door shut. "Thank God I had my cell phone in my hand."

This really sucked. I'd wasted a whole day of shopping. I'd also lost a pile of money and the gifts. And now I would have to spend a whole lot of time canceling cards and getting new ID. Right before my wedding *and* Christmas.

Not to mention replacing those car keys. "I have another set of keys at the store. Let's go there first, and I'll come back for my car later."

Nico nodded. He seemed preoccupied. He drove the Beetle down to Cannon, made a left and headed for our shops in Hess Village.

His silence concerned me. "What's up, Nico?"

"Your mom is in New York right now, right?"

"Yup. She's doing a little Christmas shopping before flying here for the wedding." Mom and Phil live in Florida. They stopped off in New York to visit his family before coming up here to be with mine.

His thin face contorted into a worried frown. "I was talking to Luca. Did you hear me before? There's a big storm expected along the eastern seaboard. It may affect all flights."

I groaned. My mother was flying in on Thursday. "Do they know when it's going to hit?"

"It's just off the Carolina coastline right now. Thing is, it looks like it will be an ice storm."

This sounded ominous. But rather fitting news on what was turning out to be a totally crap day.

* * *

We stopped for espresso and cannoli on the way to Hess Village. After that Nico dropped me off at my store, Ricci Jewelers. Tiff, working alone there this week, was wiping down counters with glass cleaner. I waved a hand as I walked by her toward the back office.

"What are you doing here?" she said, lifting her head.

"Nothing. Just getting my other set of keys from the desk." I stood in front of my office. *Crap.* My *locked* office.

"Tiff, can you open the door? I haven't got my keys."

"Sure," she said. I watched her cross the room. Tiff is Nico's younger sister, but they don't look much alike. At least, not since Nico starting bleaching his hair blond. Tiff is big into piercings, whereas Nico avoids any kind of pain. Tiff tends to wear black a lot. Nico likes wild colors. They both use the same black eyeliner though.

Once in the office, I went immediately to the desk. And stopped. And sighed.

"Can you unlock the desk too, please?"

She smiled and moved forward.

The other keys were exactly where they should be. I snatched them and shut the desk drawer.

Tiff was still standing there. Something in her manner put me on alert.

"What's the matter?"

She shifted uneasily. "Your aunt Vera called. She said Zia Sophia saw a crow."

I groaned. "Not one of her crazy omens." Zia Sophia is famous in the family. Correction. She is infamous.

Tiff shrugged. "Just passing it on. She said to tell you."

"You know she's a nutcase, Tiff."

"She thinks it has something to do with the wedding."

"Oh for—" I used my arms for emphasis. "I'm not having my wedding tainted by crackpot omens from an elderly great-aunt who clearly has reality issues. She doesn't even live here, for crissake."

Zia Sophia has never made it to the "new world." Her duty is to terrorize the Sicilian end of the family. She takes that role very seriously.

The first thing you notice about Zia Sophia? Black. Dressed in black from head to toe. She is the only one in the family who still sports the old-widow look. I've only met her once, when we visited Sicily over a decade ago. Even then, her face had the look of a wizened apple. I was never a fan of omens, so I kept my distance from her. Tiff was too young to remember much about her. But Nico was terrified of her.

"You think the distance makes a difference?" Tiff looked relieved.

"For crissake, Tiff! She saw a bird in Palermo. How the heck could it bother us here?"

Honestly. It was silly, but superstitions go back a long way, and they don't have to make a lot of sense. Crows mean bad luck in our culture. Some even think a crow is a sign that someone is going to die. We have a more liberal interpretation in the family.

For us, it usually means that something bad is going to happen.

Which is sort of redundant, because let's face it. You don't need an omen to predict that. Something bad happens to Nico and me on a weekly basis. Not to mention I'd just been robbed.

But I didn't need another thing to worry about. I waved to Tiff as I left the store.

I didn't have to walk far. The Painted Parrot was right next door. You have to know something about Nico to appreciate the name of his interior-design store. He inherited a parrot from our late great-uncle Seb a few weeks ago. The store is named after the parrot. Pauly isn't a very nice parrot, although he is colorful. He also uses very colorful language. Pauly is currently doing the country-music circuit with my best friend. Lainy McSwain and the Lonesome Doves now have a demented parrot in their act. Audiences seem to love it. But The Painted Parrot lives on in Steeltown.

The other thing about Nico is he tends to be a tad eccentric. I already mentioned the eyeliner. And the bleached-blond hair. Today he was wearing burgundy jeans with a slim black turtleneck. Not your standard blue-collar outfit in The Hammer.

As soon as he saw me, his eyes went wide. "Zia Sophia saw a crow."

I sighed. "Know it. Tiff told me."

"Do you think—"

"No, I don't think, Nico. And neither should you. Omens are ridiculous. We have other things to worry about." Real things. Like my car, and stolen purse and presents.

My phone started to sing the theme from *The Godfather* movie. That was my uncle Sammy's signature ringtone.

"Gina, I have something for you. You want to come down to the chicken coop right away."

"Um...I don't actually have my car with me at the moment."

"Why don't you—oh, never mind. Get Nico to bring you. I want to talk to him too."

Uh-oh. I clicked off.

THREE

Sammy is my favorite uncle. He is also my godfather Vince's underboss, which means a lot in The Hammer. I love them both. I hate their business. You don't get to choose your family, as I am fond of reminding my fiancé, Pete.

I do, however, get to choose my business, which is appraising and selling gemstones. As a rule, I stay way far away from the shady side. Well, I try. In this family, it's tough.

The chicken coop is less than ten miles away, so it never takes long to get there. Of course, this time Nico was driving.

"I don't understand why you drive so slow." Damn, I was irritable. Getting mugged by a skinny punk will do that to a girl.

Nico gripped the wheel in his customary fashion. Like it was a lifeline, and he had just been thrown from the *Titanic*. "Not everyone is as reckless as you are, Gina."

"I'm not reckless," I said, getting miffed. "Why does everyone say that? I don't take unnecessary risks."

Nico laughed out loud. "I'm making a list."

"Don't even go there," I warned. Last thing I needed was to be reminded of everything I had done in the past that had gone wrong. We might never make it out of the car.

Finally, we pulled onto the gravel lane leading to the cottage. Yes, it's a small two-room cottage, not a chicken coop. Years ago some relative kept chickens there.

That and a small bribe will get you a low tax bill.

The lane wasn't empty. Sammy's Mercedes was parked close to the cottage. Nico pulled up right behind it.

I opened the car door and stepped out.

"Look at all these deep ruts in the driveway," I said, trying not to turn an ankle. "What's been going on here?"

"Heavy trucks," said Nico. "I heard something about a big delivery."

Yet another thing I didn't want to know about.

We both made our way around the side. The sun was still bright, but the lake looked cold. No turquoise color here. The water was deep and dark.

I reached the screen door and pulled it open.

"Over here, Gina," said a voice.

The room was dim, lit by one light-bulb hanging on a wire from the rafters.

Coming in from brilliant sunshine made the blindness worse. I walked in a few steps and stopped to let my eyes adjust.

"Hi, Uncle Sammy," said Nico, behind me.

Sammy grunted. I could see him now, sitting at the wooden table to the side. In this poor lighting, he was a ringer for Woody Allen.

A little machine the size of a toaster perched on the table in front of him. There were several identical machines on the floor next to him.

"What's that?" I said, peering at it.

"It's a counterfeit currency finder," he said. "See? You put a bill under this light, and it will tell you if it's counterfeit or not."

I watched him demonstrate with a twenty-dollar bill.

"That one's good. See?"

I could see that it was good, but I didn't get the point. "Why do you have all these machines here?"

"It's good business, Gina," said Nico. "Banks pay a lot for these machines. So do small businesses like convenience stores. That way, they don't get stuck with a lot of fake bills."

I still didn't get it. Last I knew (and much to my regret) we were in the business of printing counterfeit money. Not selling machines to detect it.

Or were we?

"Are you still importing that counterfeit Canadian money from Canton?" I said. "I thought we were out of that business, because the quality sucked so bad."

"We are out of that business," said Sammy. "Besides. We aren't importing coffins anymore either."

The counterfeit money had been hidden in the false bottoms of several imported coffins.

"Why aren't we importing coffins— or wait. Do I really want to know?" I was pretty sure I didn't.

"The Fly By Night Funeral is currently on hold," Sammy said. "Larry, the retired embalmer at the nursing home, was apparently demented."

"No shit," said Nico, shaking his head sadly.

Sammy continued. "He was becoming a problem for the ladies, if you get my drift."

"Randy," said Nico. "Kept hiding in bedrooms and popping out to surprise them."

"Minus pajamas," Sammy added.

I groaned.

"So they cut him off Viagra. And then he tried to permanently stiffen his own weenie with—"

"Enough!" I put both hands over my ears. "Too much information."

Sammy gave a satisfied cluck. He usually knows how to make me stop asking questions.

I did a quick scan of the cabin. Now that my eyes had adjusted to the dimness, I could see something blocking the far wall. "What are those cases over there?" I asked.

"That's your wedding champagne," said Sammy. "The reception hall includes wine for the night. But Vince wanted real French champagne for everyone to toast the bride."

"Veuve Clicquot," I said, taking a closer look at the labels. "Wow. That's expensive. I'm impressed."

"He made a special deal with this importer...actually, you probably don't want to know this part," Sammy said.

He got that right.

I turned back to find Nico testing a twenty at one of the counterfeit catchers. I was still bothered by those little machines.

Why the heck would my family be in the counterfeit-detection business? I mean, how much was the markup on those little machines? Surely not enough to interest the syndicate.

Thing is, I was trained to "follow the money." There had to be money in this somehow. Real money.

Wait a minute. A light came on. *Ping!* A big humongous floodlight of a light.

"Holy shit. You're selling machines that have been fixed so they won't detect *our* counterfeit bills," I said.

Sammy grinned. It was a little creepy. "You always were a clever thing, doll."

"Genius, isn't it?" Nico said proudly. "I helped come up with the idea."

It was damned clever, I had to admit. Substitute your machine for the one in the bank. All your counterfeit bills pass the test. But the other counterfeit bills don't, so no one suspects anything.

23

Melodie Campbell

Diabolical. And really, it wouldn't hurt anyone if they didn't know about it.

Let me make this perfectly clear. I don't go in for illegal activities myself. My goal is to keep a very clean nose. So clean it's squeaky.

But as far as our family businesses go, forgery doesn't bother me overmuch. On the scale of crime, it's sort of a soft offense. Take art, for instance. If your Picasso is not by Picasso, it's still as pretty, right? (Or as ugly. I never quite got the fuss about Picasso.)

However, I realize not everyone feels that way. Banks don't, for instance. Which made me think about the next question.

"How are you getting these into—no!" I hit my hand to my forehead. "Ignore what I just said. I don't want to know."

"Are you sure, Gina? 'Cause it's really rather clever," said Nico, all excited. "We—"

24

"Stop! Don't tell me." I cut him off before he could spill it.

"As you wish, sweetheart." Sammy reached behind him. "Here's why I called. Thought you might be missing this."

He placed something familiar on the table.

"My bag!" I cried. There was my shopping bag, recently stolen. How the heck did it get here?

"Found this sitting outside the door when I came in half an hour ago," said Sammy.

I rushed over. "Is my purse inside?" Yes! There it was. I gave a sigh of relief.

"That's weird," said Nico. "Is the money gone? Credit cards?"

I retrieved the wallet and looked inside. "Credit cards are all here. The cash is missing. But I only had about thirty bucks."

"Weird that he didn't take the credit cards. Or the presents," said Nico.

"Sure is strange, dropping off everything here. Why would he do that after going through the trouble of stealing it?" I rifled through the bag to make sure all the gifts were still there. Particularly my gift for Pete. *Phew*. All there.

"Maybe he realized who you were when he checked the wallet? And didn't want to get into trouble with the family?"

"Yeah, that has to be it. But odd that he knew to deliver it here." I was really puzzled.

Sammy gave a long and telling sigh. "Here's the envelope that was left on top of it. It was addressed to you, so I haven't looked at it. But I have a suspicion."

I snatched the envelope from his hand and opened it. The note read:

Sorry, Gina. He didn't know it was you. Mario.

"SHIT!" I yelled. "That moron Mario!"

"What's it say?" Nico took the note from my hand with two fingers.

"Thought as much," said Sammy, shaking his head.

"You put Mario in charge of training the new street snatchers?" Nico started to laugh. "Oh, Sammy."

"It's not funny!" I snatched the note back from him. "Mario is a total screwup. Remember what happened with the credit-card scam?"

Mario is another cousin. Nico likes to say Mario had snuck out for a smoke when God was handing out brains. The last venture under Mario's supervision was a total disaster. You don't get very far in this business if you keep stealing credit-card numbers from your own relatives.

Sammy shrugged. "Figured he was safer doing something manual, you know? Not with numbers and names. Not so hard to screw up."

Nico grinned. "Oh, Mario will find a way. That's the one thing he's good at."

"Can you believe it? The son of a bitch had the nerve to take my cash," I said, double-checking the wallet.

"Probably wasn't Mario, Gina. Most likely it was the kid who did the snatch."

"Well, Mario should have better control of him," I shot back. "What's this family coming to, when you can't even trust your own muggers."

"You two can argue about that on your own time," said Sammy. "Nico, I need to talk to you about the other business."

That was my signal to vamoose.

"Probably I should leave the room now," I said, edging my way toward the door.

"You do that, sugar. Go look at the lake or something."

I nodded. Before I could pick up my bag and purse, he said, "Oh. I'm supposed to tell you Zia Sophia saw a crow."

"Enough about the crow already!"

"She already knows about that," said Nico.

I let the cottage door slam behind me. I walked to the bench facing the lake and sat down, putting the bag beside me. The sun was dancing off the water now. You might even be forgiven for thinking this was a lovely September day, instead of crisp December. I wound my red coat about me a little tighter and adjusted the tie belt.

Forget about crows, I told myself. *Think about the good things in your life. Like Pete. He is a great guy. You are darned lucky to be marrying him.*

Pete is a sports reporter for the *Steeltown Star*, our local newspaper. He used to be a quarterback in the majors, before a leg injury took him out. He definitely looks like a football player. Over six feet tall, he has broad shoulders and dark blond hair. You hardly notice the slight limp, because the rest of him is so fit.

He works out regularly in my cousin Luca's boxing gym.

Luckily, he has a good sense of humor. You need one if you are going to survive this family.

Now that I was getting married, maybe I could actually leave the family business behind for good. Hey! I could change my last name. Did people still do that?

It was a start. Gina Malone. That sounded pretty good. It didn't sound like a mob goddaughter at all.

Nico came around the bench. His red-and-silver ski jacket gleamed in the sun. Nico doesn't ski. He just likes the colorful jackets that come with the sport.

He sat down beside me, looking worried.

"Gina, I might need your help," he said.

I groaned. So much for leaving the family business behind.

FOUR

My cell phone sang "Shut Up and Drive." "That's Pete," I said to Nico. "Do you mind?"

He smiled and shook his head.

Pete said, "Just had a strange invitation. Your uncle Vince wants to meet me for lunch. Should I be worried?"

I gulped and said, "Just a sec." Then I signaled to Nico. "Vince wants to meet Pete for lunch," I said in a low voice.

Nico frowned. "It could be something totally innocent, Gina."

"You think?" I said. The words *Vince* and *innocent* didn't work well in the same sentence.

"Most likely he's going to give Pete the 'welcome to the family' speech. You know the one. 'You hurt our Gina, and I'll break both your legs.'"

"That's more like it," I said, turning back to the phone.

"I heard that," said Pete.

"So not a bad thing," I said, hoping it wasn't. "Don't skip this. You really have to meet him, Pete."

"I'm going to," Pete said. I could hear the obvious amusement in his voice. "We're meeting at La Paloma tomorrow. Sort of interested to see who else will be there."

"You be careful, Pete," I warned.

"I can take care of myself, babe." His voice was low and sultry.

Man, did I love this guy.

I rang off.

"What now?" said Nico.

"I suppose we should go rescue my car."

***

It was sitting there just where I had left it, waiting for me. What a relief.

Today was Wednesday, and we had wedding errands to do. We dropped Nico's car back at the store, because I insisted on driving. It was easier on my stress levels.

"What first?" I asked.

"Let's see. We need to double-check flowers, linens, the cake—"

Before Nico could finish, a phone chirped. Mine doesn't do that, so I wasn't surprised to see Nico reach for the phone on his belt.

"It's Mad Magda," he said, looking at the screen. His voice held a question. I looked over with interest.

"You're kidding," I said. Mad Magda is one of the more colorful members of our family. She is also one of the oldest. She and her geriatric lover, Jimmy the Cat, helped me out with a little job recently. Yes, I know I said that as a rule I avoid the family businesses. It's complicated.

Nico gasped. "Oh no. How awful. Of course we'll come right away. Yes. Yes. On our way." He clicked off, and his black-rimmed eyes were wide. "Jimmy's had a heart attack. We need to go there immediately. She needs help."

"Yikes! Of course," I said as we tromped over to my car. "So the retirement home? Or should we go directly to the hospital?"

"No," said Nico. "They were on an outing. It's a little out of the way." He gave me directions.

I pulled into the right lane to turn. "I hope she called 9-1-1 first," I said.

"She's calling it now," said Nico.

Weird, I thought. Why would she phone Nico before calling 9-1-1?

Ten minutes later, we were still driving.

"Are you sure she said past Caledonia?"

Nico nodded. "I know the route."

"*What* route? Route to where?"

"The truck route," said Nico.

"Huh?" This didn't seem like a normal seniors' outing. And besides, neither Jimmy nor Magda had a car. They didn't drive anymore. So what the heck was going on?

He seemed a bit fidgety. "I didn't want to tell you, Gina. I know you don't like to hear about...um...family business."

I groaned. "Oh no. Do *not* tell me. I don't want to know."

"Except I think you might have to this time. There's the truck. Pull up there, behind the ambulance." Nico pointed with a thin finger.

I parked, and Nico was out of the car before I could open my door.

Jimmy was already on a stretcher. I rushed over in time to see paramedics lift the stretcher into the back of the ambulance. His eyes were closed, and his face was contorted in pain.

Magda came up to us right away.

"Thank God you're here, Nico. And Gina." She clutched Nico's arm. Magda looked so worried, I wanted to hug her. "I have to go with Jimmy. Here are the keys to the truck. Can you...?"

"Of course," said Nico, taking the keys. "You go with Jimmy. Do they think he'll be okay?"

"Don't know yet," said Magda. She climbed into the back of the ambulance with surprising agility for a gal over seventy-five. "I'll phone."

Within seconds the ambulance had pulled away. We both stared at it careering down the road with lights and siren on.

I pulled my red coat tighter around me. It was getting chillier out. Or maybe that was the feeling in my chest.

"He was driving the truck when the heart attack came on," said Nico. "Magda managed to work the brake, or there could have been a horrible accident."

I shivered. How horrible. Poor Magda. And poor Jimmy!

"So what do we do now?" I said. "Call someone to get the truck?"

"Er...no," said Nico. "I said we'd take care of it."

"You WHAT?" I looked over at the thing. It was a midsized transport with ten wheels, not a freaking pickup truck.

"It was the least I could do, considering the state Jimmy was in, Gina. Magda can't drive anymore. They took away her license, remember? And she should be with Jimmy anyways."

That was true. They had been together for years. Actually, decades. It was hard to imagine one without the other.

I banished the thought from my mind.

But that left another problem. I frowned at the truck. This wasn't a good idea. Trucks move merchandise. That's their purpose. This was a family truck, so it stood to reason that the merchandise might be a little warm. Okay, sizzling.

Did I want to be seen escorting a truck full of hot merchandise? I did not.

"Nico, do you really need me for this? Remember, I am allergic to anything illegal." It's true. I would look terrible in an orange jumpsuit.

"*Please*, Gina. I promised her. There's no one else I can think of to call. Mario and Luca are busy with…well, never mind that. And we can't leave it here."

He had a point. We couldn't leave it here at the side of the road. It was sort of obvious. Any minute the police might drive by and notice it. Yes, I try to avoid being involved in family business. But cop business is worse.

Cops usually don't bother a truck sailing down the road, doing its own thing.

The sooner we got this over with, the better.

I relented. "Okay. So we take the truck back to wherever it came from."

"We're nearly to the drop-off point. Better to take it there. But there is a minor issue."

I stiffened. When Nico says "minor issue," I brace for the worst.

FIVE

N ico gazed over at all ten wheels. "This is a really big truck."

"Yes," I said, becoming suspicious.

"I've never driven a big truck like this before."

"What?" I said. "You're kidding me. How did you get out of all the family training?"

He shifted uneasily on his feet. "Not all. That just wasn't my thing, Gina. Remember, I was the family break-and-enter trainee. I was busy learning the ropes from Jimmy the Cat when you were getting the vehicle training."

Like most kids, we had to learn the family business when young. Really, it's not much different than a family that owns, say, a variety store or gas station. The kids are trained to help out with the family business after school, before they can decide they want a different career.

I wanted a different career. Nico was not so picky—at least, not at first.

I forced myself back to the matter at hand.

Nico nodded. "I'll do anything you want for a month. Even clean your room."

"Nico, that worked when we were kids. It doesn't work now." But he had me smiling, as he knew he would.

It had been years since I'd driven a transport. I gazed over at the thing. It stood there, almost like it was beckoning. Like it was daring me.

I wasn't very good at ignoring dares. The challenge called to me. There was just one thing.

I turned to face him. "First, come clean."

"What do you mean?" Nico said, looking off in the distance.

Like he didn't know what I meant.

"What's in the truck?"

"Oh, *that*." He pawed the ground with the toe of his sneaker. "Nothing bad. Honest."

Having been part of this family for thirty years, I know when it is in my interest to probe deeper.

"Define *bad*," I said, crossing my arms.

"I'm telling the truth. There's nothing stolen in that truck. Scout's honor."

He held up two fingers. They were the wrong two fingers. Nico never was a Boy Scout. They don't have badges for hot-wiring cars.

"Open the back," I said, standing firm.

Nico sighed deeply. He walked over to the back of the truck and hopped up on the tailgate. I watched as he worked the levers to open the doors.

I waited until he jumped down and then took a look in the back myself.

"Bottles. Cases and cases of bottles...of what?"

"Nothing dangerous, Gina."

I got close enough to see the label on one. From a distance, the other labels looked to be the same.

"Gordon's gin. Why are we shipping so many bottles of Gordon's gin?" I didn't get it. Something was amiss. Now, if I could just think...

"It's not really—" Nico stopped and took a breath. "We're just doing somebody a favor. That's all."

Why would Jimmy and Magda be driving a truck full of—

"Holy shit!" I said. "Are we back into BOOTLEGGING?"

Nico squirmed like a little kid. "Well, technically, we were never *not* in it, Gina. We never really left it."

"Oh for crissake." I felt my heart pound.

Here's the thing about our past. Bootlegging is the way my family got started in their various businesses. You might say it provided the seed money.

The Hammer is pretty close to the American border. So when Prohibition came about, my great-grandfather and his buddies got busy. Or was it my great-great? Doesn't matter. Thing is, they were pretty good at making gin, and even better at sneaking it across the border.

"I thought all the stills had been shut down before we were born," I said, waving my arms in the air.

Nico shrugged. "You can still make a lot of money bypassing taxation, Gina. But really, it's a very secondary business for us."

I still had a whole lot of questions. But I was starting to feel that I shouldn't ask them. The less I knew, the better.

"Nico, this is a really bad idea," I said. "Can't we just call someone else to move this truck? I don't want to be this involved."

"We're not going far. Honestly, Gina, we can get the truck to its destination in almost the same time it would take you to track down someone to do it instead of us. And I can't let Magda down. I promised we'd take care of it."

"This sucks," I grumbled. That was the problem. I hated to let people down, especially Jimmy and Magda. They had helped me a few weeks back with the whole art-gallery heist. Actually, it was a reverse heist. But I'm not sure the cops would see it that way.

Poor Jimmy. I hoped he was doing okay. Yes, I'd do this for him. I mean, let's be realistic. We were nearly at the destination. What could possibly go wrong at this stage?

"Hand me the keys," I said. "Are you going to come with me or drive my car?"

"Drive your car, so we can leave immediately after we do the drop-off."

I winced as I tossed him my second set
of keys. I really don't like terms like *do the
drop-off*.

SIX

One cool thing I discovered. Driving a transport truck is like riding a bicycle. It didn't take me long to remember how to get the thing in gear and start shifting up. Steering was as I remembered. It was a beast, compared to my frisky little car.

Nico led the way, driving my car. About five minutes later we pulled into a small, deserted plaza. It had a convenience store, a tobacco shop and a small garage with one gas pump.

I may have mentioned that I am writing a book, *Burglary for Dummies*. Nico is helping me edit it. I was pleased to see that he carefully executed the instructions in chapter 17: *Always park around the back.*

Me, I couldn't do that because of the length of the transport. Luckily, this place was set up for trucks, so I was able to pull in without having to execute a sharp turn. I took the beast all the way to the end of the lot, keeping away from the shops.

Nico was already coming around the side when I got the truck stopped. In the process of getting out of the cab, I discovered something. This is definitely a situation where you want to dress for the occasion. I don't recommend a long wraparound coat and high heels.

Nico didn't notice when I fell out of the cab. He was already galloping over to meet someone.

"Hi, Danny!" he said.

From my vantage point on the ground, I could see a young man approaching.

He had a wide grin on his face. The dude was super slim with nice brown eyes and black hair that went halfway down his back. He wore jeans and a worn brown-suede jacket.

"Nico!" They embraced like old friends. Kind of weird, I guess, for guys to embrace, but we're Italian, and Nico is Nico.

When they separated, Nico said, "Gina, this is Danny Brant. This is my cousin Gina, Danny."

Danny watched me struggle to my feet. He gave me a big smile. "Heard about you." He had a soft tenor voice. "You got a rep and a half in this burg."

"It's nothing," I said modestly, brushing gravel dust off my coat. *Wait a minute.* Why was I—

"They call you Mini Mags," said Danny.

"They WHAT?" Oh crap. People were comparing me to Mad Magda?

"No shit," said Nico, eyes wide and excited. "That's top of the league."

"I'm not—oh for crissake," I said. Mad Magda is a legend in the world of cat burglary. I'm not in that class *at all*. I'm not even in the same school district.

"The Lone Rearranger and Mini Mags. We're getting famous, Gina!"

I watched in horror as Nico and Danny high-fived each other.

I didn't want to be famous. I didn't want to have a rep of any sort. And I sure as hell didn't want to spend any more time than I had to with a truck full of bootlegged hooch.

"Em, can we get going here?" I said. "I'm getting married in three days, and there's sort of a lot to do."

"Sure, Gina. Let's go inside, Danny." Nico and Danny led the way into the building, and I followed. Nobody else seemed to be around. Danny led us through the tobacco shop to a little office off the back.

"Can I use the washroom?" I asked.

"It's right over there." Danny pointed.

I didn't really need to go. But I wanted to get away from any paperwork business Nico and Danny were conducting. The less I knew about this new aspect of family affairs, the better. Well, new to me anyway.

Bootlegging. Who'da thunk it? Talk about retro.

I killed some time in the bathroom, which was surprisingly clean and pretty. The walls were painted a light peach. A wallpaper accent border circled the room, just under the ceiling. Someone had provided a bowl of cinnamon-scented potpourri for the counter.

First thing I did was check my cell phone. Two texts, from Luca and Mario, both about crows.

Also while in there, I spent a few minutes thinking about the events of that morning. It hadn't started well. Getting mugged in your hometown is not a banner way to begin the day. It's doubly bad when you are a member of the local crime family. Off the charts when it's your own family mugging you. If this ever got out, our entire family reputation would be toast with marmalade. I could just imagine my crappy distant cousins in Buffalo howling about it.

No question, I wasn't breathing a word of this to anyone.

I slung my purse across my chest. Just when I'd decided it was probably safe to come out of the washroom, the yelling started.

SEVEN

"The truck! Gina, the truck!"

I dashed out of the complex to find Nico running across the parking lot. He came to a full stop. Then he sank down on the gravel with a dramatic groan. I moved my eyes from him to the empty spot in front of him.

The truck gave a final *toot* goodbye. We all watched the back end of it pull onto the highway.

"They stole the truck." Nico groaned again. "Are you sure Zia Sophia didn't see two crows?"

"SHIT!" I yelled, throwing my arms in the air. This was definitely a day beyond crap. "But who?"

"Didn't see," said Danny. "Heard the engine start and rushed out here, but..."

"They were already pulling away," said Nico. He moaned like he was in pain.

"Wait a minute. Why are we waiting here? Nico, we have to go after it! Come on!" I turned on my heel and took off. I raced toward the back of the strip plaza. Nico and Danny were close behind me.

My car was right there, waiting. We all climbed in and slammed the doors.

I did a record three-point turn and was on the highway in seconds.

"Can you see it?" I said, squinting through the windshield.

"Just barely," said Danny. He pointed with a finger. "Straight down the highway, up ahead. There are a few cars in between us."

I stepped on the gas. Nico groaned in response.

"How did they even get it started? I have the keys right here." I checked to make sure that my purse was still slung across my shoulder.

"They have ways," said Danny in his laconic way.

"*Who* has ways? Who would even do such a thing? It was a family truck! Is this guy insane?" You have to be nuts to steal anything from our family. Everyone knows that. And this was a big hulking truck full of...let's say, merchandise.

"What am I going to tell Magda?" Nico was rocking back and forth, holding his head in his hands.

"Forget about Magda. What are we going to tell Uncle Vince? It's his truck!" I said, gripping the steering wheel with both hands.

You have to know my godfather, Uncle Vince, to fully understand that sentence.

Let me try to explain. You know how Dr. Who is a Time Lord? My uncle Vince is a Crime Lord.

Suffice it to say, you don't want to cross him.

"Actually, it's Aunt Miriam's truck. All the vehicles are in her name," Nico said. "For tax reasons."

"Oh freakin' hell," I said with a shiver. That made it way worse. Even my godfather doesn't mess with Aunt Miriam.

"He's slowing down," Danny said, pointing. "That's Hagersville up ahead. You have to slow down to sixty."

"Good," I said with satisfaction. "We'll catch up."

"And do what?" Nico's voice rose an octave. "Exactly what are you planning to do, Gina? Hit them over the head with your purse?"

"I'm not letting them get away," I growled.

"I'm calling Sammy," Nico said. He unhooked his phone and punched some numbers.

"You can call whoever you like, but I'M NOT LETTING THEM GET AWAY!"

Nope, I was fed up. Like, totally. Everybody was taking advantage of me these days, and I wasn't going to put up with it anymore.

First, I get mugged by that totally skinny dude. And now those bastards steal my truck. I *hate* being made a fool of. They were going to pay, man. I was gritting my teeth something fierce.

"What are you mumbling, Gina?" said Nico. Then he turned his attention to the phone. "Oh, hi, Sammy. We got a situation here."

"They're going into that Tim Hortons parking lot," said Danny from the backseat.

"Yup...Yup...We're at the Tim Hortons in Hagersville," said Nico into the phone.

"No, they're pulling around the corner so they don't have to go into the parking lot," said Danny, all eager.

"I see it," I said.

I booted it up to the light, ready to turn. Doors opened on the truck cab, and two big guys heaved themselves out. They had long black hair and each weighed at least a hundred pounds more than necessary.

"Uh-oh," said Danny. "Those are really bad hombres. I know them. You don't want to mess with them, Gina."

"They don't want to mess with me," I mumbled. No kidding. I was having a really bad day.

"Gina, Sammy wants to talk to you." Nico held the phone over to me.

"Sammy can freaking well wait," I said.

I pulled up and screeched to a halt right behind the truck. The two bad guys were out of sight now, getting their donuts and coffees inside. Conveniently, they had left the truck running.

"Move over to the driver's seat and follow me," I shouted to Nico. "Keep your cell phone on."

I pushed open my door and vaulted out.

"Hey, Gina, what..." Nico's voice trailed off behind me.

In ten seconds I was at the truck. Another five and I had the driver's door open. I threw myself up into the driver's seat and gave the door a good slam. Before I could get the truck in gear, the passenger door opened. Danny slid in and said, "Get moving! I think they saw us."

I stumbled getting the truck into first. Then the thing jumped as only big hulking monsters that carry massive amounts of bootleg shit can do. "CRAP!" I yelled, then tried again and managed first.

I was vaguely aware of a commotion outside. Honestly, I was putting all my concentration into getting the damned vehicle moving.

Bang!

"Holy shit, they're shooting at us!" said Danny. He dove under the dash.

Bang, bang!

"They're freaking nuts!" yelled Danny.

Two bullets hit the box or the cab. I couldn't tell which and figured it wasn't a good time to check.

I went through gears like they were disposable. More shots rang out behind us. The truck shot from the shoulder onto the highway, quickly followed by a little silver car—my car. With Nico at the wheel.

We bolted down the highway, totally ignoring the speed signs. I could barely hear the gunshots now.

For some weird reason, I felt elated. "We did it!" I said to Danny. "We stole the truck back!"

"I am thinking this isn't going to end well," said Danny, poking his head up.

"Oh, don't be such a wuss," I said. "We whupped their asses." *Ha! Take that, universe. Gina Gallo is back in black.* I couldn't wipe the grin off my face. My confidence was back again. Reclaiming a hijacked transport from a bunch of thugs will do that to a girl.

We drove for a few miles at a pace somewhat over the speed limit. I checked the side mirror of the truck. No cars following us. The coast was clear.

I was still feeling my high.

"We seem to be heading toward Brantford," said Danny as another signpost passed by.

"What's in Brantford?" I asked quite innocently.

"No idea. I'm just pointing it out, as we seem to be going away from the place where this truck was supposed to end up."

"Rats," I said, remembering our purpose. "So you want me to turn around?" I had no idea where to turn around. This was Grade A farmland. Not a crossroad in sight.

"You know what? I can take it from here," Danny said. "I know the drop-off point."

"Really? You can drive this rig?"

Danny grinned. He really was nice-looking, with beautiful brown eyes. "I can drive it. My family is into tobacco farming. I drive those trucks all the time."

"What a relief! If I stop here, is it okay?"

Danny nodded.

I signaled right, so Nico would know what I had in mind. Then I slowed down and maneuvered the truck onto the shoulder. Nico pulled up behind me. We all got out of the vehicles. This time I managed to stay on my feet instead of rolling onto the gravel. Nico came running to meet us.

"Danny is going to take it from here," I said.

Just then my cell phone rang with Pete's signature tune. "Hang on a sec," I said to Nico and Danny.

"HELLO," I yelled into it.

"Whoa, babe. Not so loud."

I tried to steady my voice. "Sorry. I'm outside, and there's a lot of noise."

"Where are you?"

I gulped. Logical question. I needed a logical answer, quick.

"I'm helping Nico make a delivery. From the store." Well, it was half true. I didn't mention that we had recently been through a hail of bullets and were now parked by the side of the road in the middle of nowhere.

"You know it's nearly six. We were going to have dinner together before the bachelor party."

Six! Crap. "Sorry, Pete. The time got away from us." I signaled frantically to Nico.

Then I used that hand to cover the phone. "It's the bachelor party tonight!" I said to Nico.

Nico's eyes popped. "I was supposed to pick up Pete."

I uncovered the phone. "I'm thinking you might want to take a taxi, Pete. We're sort of running late and will be stuck here for a bit."

"No problem. I'll get a cab."

I said goodbye and turned back to the boys. Nico and Danny were doing that hug thing again.

"Thanks a mil, Danny. For everything," said Nico, pulling back.

"We owe you for this," I added.

"No probs." Danny smiled and shrugged his narrow shoulders.

"Let me know if we can ever do anything for you," I said. "I mean that." And I did.

Danny shoved his hands into his jean pockets and looked off in the distance. "You're my friends."

EIGHT

We waited until Danny had the truck in gear. When it set off down the road, Nico and I got into my car.

"Isn't she great?" said Nico.

I was confused. "What, the car?"

"No, silly. Danny."

She? Danny was a she?

Well, that explained the gorgeous cheekbones.

"Gina, I know this is last-minute. But can I bring Danny to the wedding?"

"Sure," I said, my tone bright. "One more won't break the budget. Just make sure to let Aunt Vera know, for numbers."

What a day for surprises. As we pulled onto the highway, I could almost feel his happiness.

The bachelor party was at the Knights of Columbus hall. I pulled up in front to let Nico out. Three thugs were standing on the sidewalk, having a smoke. Unfortunately, they spotted me. So I did the friendly thing. I got out of the car with Nico to say hi.

"Hey, Gina," said Joey. He actually looked happy to see me. "Looking forward to the big day?"

I grinned back. "Can't wait for it to be over. Would you want Aunt Miriam running *your* wedding?"

His tank of a body did a little shiver. I knew it would. Mere mention of that name has a terrifying effect on the men in our family.

Joey is a distant cousin of mine from Buffalo. At one time, he would have liked to be a "kissing cousin." That wasn't going to happen. Even then I was fussy about my men. Thugs didn't make the list.

Bertoni had his usual sneer on. He is as skinny as Joey is solid. It is said in the family that Joey could bench-press a Volvo station wagon. Even with Bertoni sitting in it.

Lou was the third goon of the bunch. He is okay. Not too much in the brain department, but he is big on respect. Since the art-gallery reverse heist of last month, I am riding high in the family.

"Where's Carmine?" I said. He is the last of my degenerate Yankee cousins and the worst of the bunch.

"Still in New York. Coming with Big Sally and the rest on Friday."

I nodded with a forced smile. I keep my distance from Big Sally, who heads up the New York branch of the family. With any luck, they wouldn't get here because of the storm.

And I could seriously do without Carmine. The rat-faced fink had nearly bankrupted me a few months back by pulling a rotten scheme while babysitting my store. I got him back but good, and it has been an uneasy truce ever since. While I don't generally approve of blackmail as a career choice, it has its uses.

"Lainy coming to the wedding?" Bertoni asked.

"Of course. She's my maid of honor. She'll be here on Friday." All the boys have a thing for my best friend, Lainy. You may have heard of her. Lainy McSwain and the Lonesome Doves were currently singing in Vegas. They were topping the country charts with their new hit "You're Roadkill on My Highway of Life."

"Will she be singing at the reception?" asked Lou, all excited.

"That's the plan. See you all on Saturday," I said. "Have fun tonight."

I gave a little wave as I took off.

On the way home to my condo, I thought about the whole male-bonding thing. Pete said bachelor parties weren't really his thing. I believed him, but I didn't mind him going to this one. It would give him a chance to bond with my male relatives. This was a good thing, because they really don't welcome a whole lot of outsiders into the family. And you really do want to be welcomed, believe me. The alternative is unpleasant. A few of the non-welcomed are now swimming with the fishes in Burlington Bay.

Besides, he couldn't really get out of going to his own bachelor party. Guy parties like these were a big excuse to gamble, drink too much and eat all kinds of junk food.

Also, a lot of business was conducted at these things. Pete would avoid that part. But I knew him well, and he would hold his own with the gambling and drinking. It was a good thing he's a big lad with an Irish constitution.

Man, I was exhausted. All I wanted to do was get home, have a quick supper and take a long bath. That wasn't asking too much, was it?

The gods hate me.

* * *

I pulled into the driveway and my usual parking spot. I grabbed my purse from the passenger seat and climbed wearily out of the car.

"Well, well. Look who's here," said a familiar voice.

Crap. It was Spence. Tall, skinny Spence. The creepy guy who once had a crush on me in high school. Now a cop in The Hammer and my personal nemesis. Could this week get any worse?

"Gina Gallo, the girl with the longest confession. Who just happened to be involved in a gunfight in Hagersville. What a coincidence."

Gulp. "What are you doing here, Spence?"

"Following up on that gunfight. You were seen. I figured you'd turn up here eventually," he said.

"What gunfight? Don't be ridiculous. This isn't the Wild West." I forced a smile. "Besides, I don't even own a gun."

"Then what about these bullet holes here in your fender?"

"What?" I hoofed it around to where he was standing. *Holy shit.* There were three holes in the back passenger-side fender. I hadn't seen them when I got in on the driver's side.

"Freakin' hell!" I said, throwing my arms in the air. "They shot up my car!" Now I was mad.

"*Who* shot up your car?" said Spence, folding his arms across his chest.

"Don't know," I said, going in for a closer look at the holes. "Two big guys. Don't know them personally."

"I'll bet you don't."

"Give me a break, Spence! I've had a really bad day." No kidding. Not to mention it was the first time I've ever been shot at. "Besides, how did you even know it was me?"

"Got a report about a hijacking and gunfire at a Tim Hortons. The local cops got a description of the car from some bystanders, and the license-plate number. I recognized it. My lucky day."

Shit.

"Gina," Spence said, shaking his head. "Stealing a truck. I never expected to see you sink as low as this."

That hurt.

"I wasn't stealing it! It was *my truck*," I said, poking a finger through the air at him.

"I was merely sneaking it back from the thugs who took off with it!"

Oops.

And that's when I got hauled down to the police station.

NINE

Twenty minutes later, I was sitting on a bench in my least favorite place in The Hammer. Paulo, my slick lawyer cousin, met me there.

The bench lined one side of the room, which was the perfect place to watch Paulo's entrance. As usual, it was dramatic. Every female in the place was aware of him the second he walked into the station. Something about pheromones, I've been told. As always, he looked like he had just walked off the cover of *GQ*. Paulo scanned the room, found me and strode over.

The first thing out of his mouth was, "Zia Sophia saw a crow."

"FUCK THE STUPID CROW!" *Oops.* I might have yelled that a little too loud. Every head in the place turned.

"Watch the potty mouth, Gina. These cops have tender ears." Paulo was grinning.

Spence started over to us. His face turned to a snarl when he saw Paulo. But that was nothing compared to when Aunt Miriam came charging in seconds later.

"Jesus Christ," muttered Spence.

Aunt Miriam stood at the entrance, wearing a massive coat of sheared beaver. Her eyes were fierce. She looked this way and that. All five feet four inches of her marched into the room and took command.

"Where's that boy?" she demanded. Her mouth was fixed in a grim line. Her black helmet hair was solid, as was her sturdy body. I was never so glad to see someone.

"There you are." Her beady brown eyes fixed on Spence, who was attempting to sneak into one of the back rooms. "You come here. I wanna talk to you."

Spence froze. And I knew why.

He and my aunt were not unknown to each other. In fact, you could say there was a faint odor of blackmail in the air.

I may not have mentioned that Spence and I went to the same Catholic high school. Suffice it to say that my aunt worked there and had the dope on him. By this I don't mean drugs. I mean the stuff of adolescent embarrassment nightmares. The kind you don't want your mother to know about.

Or any of your co-workers, for that matter. Even better.

"You all right, Gina? This shameless boy bothering you?" She poked her cane at Spence, who was managing to look green.

"I'm fine," I said, enjoying the show.

Aunt Miriam turned to my older cousin. "You need help, Paulo?"

Paulo was still grinning. He shook his head. "I got this."

"Then I wait here until you say go." She parked herself on the bench beside me. It rocked dangerously.

No sooner did she plunk down than her nose started to twitch. "What's that smell?"

"Probably motor oil. I rolled in some when I fell out of the truck cab."

"Sammy tole me about the truck. You're a good girl, Gina." She patted my arm.

"How's Jimmy?" I said, remembering why I'd gotten involved in this in the first place.

"Not so good." She shook her head solemnly. "Too old to pull jobs like that anymore. But what can you tell men? So like children. Never listen."

That made me smile. I couldn't imagine anyone not listening to Aunt Miriam and living to tell about it.

"What you got in your hair, Gina?" she said. Then she reached over and pulled out something icky.

Paulo did his magic. All I had to do was give a description of the thugs who hijacked the truck and shot at me. We were out of there in five minutes. I suspect no one in the station wanted Aunt Miriam staring at them with her evil eye for longer than necessary.

I waited until we were out of the building before stating the obvious. "Before you say anything, I know about the crow."

"It was a flock of crows," she said.

Of course it was.

* * *

I dreamed about birds that night. You know that Alfred Hitchcock horror movie with Tippi Hedren?

In my dream, birds were following me everywhere, squawking at me. Little birds, big birds and one especially scary black bird that, unfortunately, reminded me of Zia Sophia. I forced myself awake when the other birds started to acquire faces.

My relatives had turned into birds.

Even I had to admit it was not a good omen.

TEN

When the phone rang at eleven the next morning, I ran for it.

"Lainy!" I yelled into it.

"How ya doin', sugar? All set for the big day?"

"You bet. Except I don't have a car right now." I explained the previous day's fiasco, including the unexpected bullet-holes incident.

"Wow, hon. You do lead an exciting life."

This, coming from a country and western star who was mobbed wherever she traveled. But that was the great thing about Lainy. She never judged you. Of course, we wouldn't have lasted long as friends otherwise. Not with my history.

"I'm flying in Friday, landing in Toronto around three," she said. "I'll rent a car at the airport and be there in plenty of time for the rehearsal. Sorry I can't stay longer. We were lucky to get this Vegas gig, and I just gotta be back for the band on Sunday night."

"You're a doll to make the trip," I said. "Can't thank you enough."

"Seriously, I wouldn't miss it, Gina. You still sure this is the fella you want?"

"I'm sure."

"Good stuff. Then it's time to rope 'im, brand 'im and bring 'im on home."

I clicked off with a big smile on my face.

* * *

It was almost noon when I got to Pete's apartment. He was sitting at the kitchen table in his underwear, counting a bunch of twenties. He didn't look too worse for wear. In fact, he looked positively spry.

"Watcha got there?" I said, kissing the top of his light-brown head.

"My winnings from the bachelor party," he said proudly. A big grin split his face. "Seven hundred bucks!"

I frowned down at the twenty-dollar bills. They looked suspiciously newish. "Em...you might want to check those to make sure they're real. I mean, you did win them off my family." I moved to the kitchen in search of coffee.

"Good point. I'll take them to the bank this afternoon," Pete said. "They have those counterfeit-catcher machines there."

I stopped abruptly with my hand reaching for the coffeepot. "Oh, right," I said feebly. "Counterfeit catchers. That should work."

Somehow I was going to have to make sure those bills only got used in The Hammer.

"How did the lunch go with Uncle Vince?" I said, pouring coffee into a mug.

"It went great," said Pete. "He just wanted to welcome me to the family. And make sure I was going to treat you right. Which, of course, I am. I'm not a fool."

I flinched. The dreaded speech. Just as I had feared.

"Better yet, look what he gave me." Pete rose from the table and disappeared into the bedroom. Seconds later he came back gripping an item in his right hand.

I nearly dropped the mug. "Holy crap! A handgun?"

Pete grinned. "Glock nine millimeter. All the men in the family have one," he said proudly.

"I guess they've accepted you completely then."

"Good to know." Pete turned the gun over in his hands, admiring it. "This beats the hell out of my old revolver."

I was relieved in an ambivalent sort of way. Relieved that Uncle Vince had made this gesture. Not so relieved that Pete had a new, somewhat illegal handgun in the house. Also not so thrilled that Pete seemed to be quite fond of and familiar with guns in general.

Of course, he was from Buffalo. One had to make allowances.

But guns. I wasn't so keen on guns at the moment. Which reminded me. I had to get my car to my cousin Tony's body shop before Pete noticed the bullet holes.

I made him put the gun away. Then we had a small argument about what to have for breakfast. I suggested bacon and eggs. Pete put forth a whole lot of other ideas. As usual, he won. Which means I also won, because Pete is a generous guy.

An hour later, I extricated my various body parts from his.

"What are you doing today?" he murmured from the bed.

"I have to meet Nico and the girls at the reception hall later to fill out name cards for the tables," I said. Where were my undies? Oh yeah. I could see a trail of clothes on the floor leading down the hall.

"So this is really the last time I see you before the wedding?"

"Yup," I said, picking up items of clothing as I found them. "I'm going to be really busy today and tomorrow. But I'll call you."

"Mmmph," he said.

He was asleep when I left the condo.

I was just getting into my car when Nico called.

"Jimmy's still with us. I talked to Magda."

"What a relief!" I said, truly happy to hear it. "Can we go to the hospital and visit him?"

"That's why I'm calling. Magda wants to talk to us, and she won't leave his bedside. Frankly, this makes me nervous, Gina."

I was more philosophical. "Well, we won't know more until we visit. Wait a minute. Does she know about the shootout with the truck?"

"That's one of the reasons I'm nervous."

Now I was nervous. "I'll pick you up in an hour."

I had just clicked off the phone when it rang again. This time it was Sammy.

"Gina, I think it's important you come to the chicken coop. *Now*. Bring your dippy cousin."

He clicked off. I stood staring at the phone in my hand.

Wow. That was weird. Sammy was hardly ever short with me.

I called Nico back and told him I'd pick him up in fifteen minutes instead.

* * *

When we got to the chicken coop, Sammy was pacing. This was never a good sign.

"What were you thinking, Gina? Stealing the truck back when they're armed and you're not?" His whole body was stiff with anger. "You know better. Leave it to the family, like you were trained."

I put up both hands like stop signs. "I'm sorry, Sammy. I was just so freaking mad. First the skinny dude mugged me. Then these scumbags took off with my truck. I was sick and tired of people taking advantage of me, and I just reacted." Okay, over-reacted. "Besides, I didn't know they were carrying. I'm not stupid."

"It's true, Sammy," said Nico. "We had no idea they were carrying until we heard the gunshots."

Sammy came over and gave me a big hug. "I was all shook up when I heard. Don't ever do that again, you hear me? You'll give me a heart attack. " He kissed me on the cheek, then pushed back.

"Oh god, that reminds me. I should call Magda," said Nico. "We're a little later than I said we'd be." Nico worked his speed dial.

Probably that should have been a clue. Things might have worked out differently if I had been thinking straight. If I hadn't been so preoccupied with weddings and black birds, maybe I would have been sharper and stopped to consider why Nico had Jimmy the Cat and Mad Magda on speed dial.

"Hey, Magda, Jimmy still good?…That's even better news…Yeah…Yeah…Okay… You really think so?…But I mean, Bertoni? And Lou?…All right, if you say so…Yup, we'll be by later. *Ciao ciao.*" He clicked off.

"Jimmy's going to pull through," he said. "The doctors are optimistic for a good recovery."

"Great!" I said, truly relieved. "What was all that about Bertoni and Lou?"

Nico shifted uncomfortably. "Magda wanted us to do something for her and

Jimmy, but it was time sensitive. So she got Bertoni and Lou to do it instead."

I snorted. "Those losers? Why would she ever choose them?"

"Joey and Mario are busy with the bank project," Nico said.

Bank project? What bank project? Were we pulling a bank job? Holy crap, and then I remembered. The counterfeit-catcher-exchange plan.

Phew.

"What did she need done, Nico?" Sammy looked up from the table.

"Er…" Nico was hedging. I could see it. "You know that project they have going in the basement of the, um, building."

"Fly By Night Funerals?" I said.

"No, doll," said Sammy. "The funeral-home business is shutting down."

"That's a relief," I said. It was pretty hard to hide an illegal funeral home. Too many dead bodies going in and out.

People were liable to become suspicious. Though I had to admit, the branding had been superb. *You plug 'em, we plant 'em* had a certain ring to it, besides being the truth.

"So what's the new business about?" I said. They both squirmed.

"Thought you would have figured that out by now, Gina," Sammy said.

Okay, that made me feel crummy. Was I losing my touch? I looked over at Nico. He wasn't connecting.

Sammy said, "Nico, I'm thinking you should get over there anyway. It *is* Bertoni and Lou we're talking about, after all."

Sammy appeared to be worried. The lines were etched deeper than usual on his face.

"You're right," said Nico, snapping to attention. "Come on, Gina. We need to get moving."

Oh great, I thought to myself. *More involvement. Yippee.*

ELEVEN

"Where are we going?" I said to Nico when we got into my car.

"The reception hall. You remember. Aunt Pinky and some of the others are decorating for the wedding, and I promised we'd be there to help."

This was strange. I'd thought we had to be checking something out for Jimmy and Magda.

It occurred to me, since I was already involved up to my neck, that I might as well get the whole story. So when we pulled into the laneway leading to the reception hall, I stopped the car and cornered Nico. "Does this new business have anything to do with the truck that got hijacked?"

"Technically, it wasn't hijacked, Gina. We weren't in the thing when they stole it."

"Don't change the subject. Does this involve the cargo we were moving?"

"It might," he said cryptically.

"Come on, Nico. Give!"

He sighed. "You remember the Last Chance Club from the retirement home."

"Of course," I said. Who could forget their main event, speed dating for geezers?

"Well, remember they all wanted to take a bus trip to Vegas but couldn't afford it? That's what the underground funeral home was all about. They wanted to raise money to play the tables."

"I get it, Nico. Embalming for dollars. Continue."

"Right. Well, they tried another tack to raise money." Nico turned to look at me. "You have to realize that these people are really old, Gina. They remember the old ways. Fondly."

Old ways. Okay. I could buy that. But what...?

"Oh. My. God. They're the bootleggers!" Sweet Jimmy and dear Magda. Channeling the 1920s right here in The Hammer. I started to giggle.

"Jimmy found the old family recipe for grappa. He went to Vince for permission, and Vince has been bankrolling the operation. Those bottles in the truck were grappa, not gin."

"So my godfather is the bootlegger?" Well, that was fitting. Just like his grandfather before him.

"He's the money behind it. Jimmy and Magda are the managers. Joey and Mario are the muscle."

Well, they sure weren't the brains.

I put the car back in gear and continued along the laneway.

The Forum is a typical Italian banquet hall. By this I mean it is extremely over-decorated and gaudy.

Several Roman columns line the drive. As you drive up to the entrance, a huge fountain greets you. The fountain has several marble cherubs frolicking about in it. If you look closely, you can see water spurting out of their wee-wees. You really don't want to look that close.

The building itself is a mixture of Roman temple architecture and over-the-top baroque. My relatives don't believe in doing anything halfway. Yes, the family owns it.

I parked in the reserved parking out front. There were four cars there already, including my aunt Pinky's Lexus.

"Good," said Nico, noticing the Lexus. "That means the others will be here too."

"What others?" I said. But Nico was already out of the car and making for the stairs.

There are a lot of steps leading up to the main double doors. You can't miss the doors. They are painted gold. Not yellow. Gold.

If the doors fail to impress, wait until you open them.

"We're in the Venetian Ballroom," said Nico. "I can't wait for you to see it."

Nico grasped one of the gold handles and pulled. I walked into the foyer and was immediately blinded by sparkly light dancing off a wall of mirrors.

The Forum has a huge ballroom and a smaller banquet hall. So theoretically, two events can take place at one time. Not so for my wedding. We would have the whole building to ourselves. This was more a safety precaution than anything else. A lot of, shall we say, important people were going to be at my wedding. Big Sally, for one. The security would be top-notch.

The event rooms are on the main floor, which has an impressive twenty-foot ceiling. The kitchens and storage rooms are on the floor below. The land slopes downward at the back, so you can make deliveries without having to bother with stairs.

I walked past the tacky Greek plaster statues and the busts of Roman emperors. The Venetian Ballroom was straight ahead.

"Wait," Nico called after me. "I want this to be a surprise. Close your eyes before you walk in."

I sighed and closed my eyes. Nico was always one for the dramatic. He took my arm and guided me into the room.

"You can open them now," he said.

I obeyed. Then looked. Then gasped. "Oh my god, Nico, this is *fab*!"

"You like it?" I could hear the happiness in his voice.

"I love it!" I clapped my hands together. Yes, it was over the top. But done in such a cheerful way that you couldn't help but smile.

Nico had gone to town with the black-and-pink theme. Draperies of shimmering hot pink fell from rods high on the ceiling to pool on the floor. About thirty round tables for eight were set up. Each was draped with a black tablecloth. Silver cutlery and chargers gleamed under the many enormous chandeliers. Bright-pink linen napkins puffed out of every wineglass on the table.

The centerpieces were concoctions of mirror, crystal and more hot pink. I could see flower vases rising up from the center to magnificent heights. Everything sparkled as sunlight cascaded in from the palladian windows.

"Wait until we get the flowers," said Nico. "And the ice sculptures. That will really pull it all together."

Ice sculptures. I had to grin. Well, at least it wasn't the pink flamingos I had been half expecting.

"Have you seen the head table?" Nico said.

I turned my gaze to the right. The head table was a reverse of the others. Black draperies framed the rectangular table. A pink tablecloth ran the length of it, with a glittering silver runner down the middle. Instead of centerpieces, the table had two enormous silver candelabras at each end. No kidding. Those candle holders had to be four feet high.

"It's gorgeous, Nico. I truly do love it," I said.

"Hi, Gina!" Pinky was walking across the parquet dance floor. Did I mention a dance floor? Yes, the room is huge. You could seat 250 people for dinner and not have to move tables afterward for dancing.

"Hasn't Nico done a fabulous job?" She rushed right up to me and planted a kiss on either cheek. Then she did the time-honored thing of wiping her lipstick off my cheek with her thumb. She moved on to Nico next.

My aunt Pinky lived up to her name. That was a fuchsia wool Versace dress she was wearing. Pinky is a former beauty queen who still looks the part. She is the youngest of my mother's sisters.

"Oh! Before I forget. Gina, I don't want to alarm you, but Rosina in Palermo told Vera that Zia Sophia has seen a—"

"Crow! I know. I'm dealing with it." That was a lie. I wasn't dealing with it well at all.

"Come into the bridal room," Pinky said to me. "We're working on place cards there."

"I need to go check something," said Nico. "Be back in a bit."

I dutifully followed Pinky into the bridal room, which was a special room off to the left, set aside for the bride and her attendants. It was over-the-top fluffy, dripping lace and satin. In fact, one might mistake it for a Victorian bordello.

Three very old ladies were seated around a glass table. It held a pile of lists and name cards.

"Gina!" said my great-aunt Rita. "You see? We all came to help."

And there they were, the female contingent of the Last Chance Club from the Holy Cannoli Retirement Home. Minus Mad Magda, of course, who was at the hospital with Jimmy.

I started around the table to give my kisses. Great-Aunt Rita first, then Mrs. Pesce and Loose Trudy.

About Loose Trudy. Don't ask. I did, and I'm scarred for life.

"Thanks for helping. You're all wonderful to come here." It was the right thing to say.

I watched as they settled back in their chairs, each smiling broadly.

What a bunch of old dears. They looked so sweet in their colorful pastel tracksuits. You'd never know they were all retired ex-mobsters who had done time for armed robbery.

"So you bagged yourself a big one," said Loose Trudy. "I like the big ones." She giggled.

"You like anything that comes with a wiener," said Mrs. Pesce. Her pug face was set to disapproval.

"Sausage, Jeanie. Big round sausage. Wieners are for sissies."

"Behave yourself, girls," Great-Aunt Rita ordered. "This here is a solemn occasion. Ain't every day a mob goddaughter gets married."

"I'm not a—" I started to protest. "Well, okay. Technically, I am. But not practicing," I added.

"She's had enough practice," snorted Loose Trudy. "Them Loan Rearranger burglaries and all."

Oh for crissake. Would I never live those down?

"Gina? Can you come downstairs with me for a minute?" Nico popped his head around the doorframe. His eyes were wide and frightful.

I looked over at Pinky, who shrugged. "Go," she said. "We'll be here for a while."

TWELVE

I followed Nico out of the ballroom and to the main hall. He was really hoofing it.

"Wait up!" I yelled when he got to the stairs at the side of the building. "What's this all about?"

"You've got a major in chemistry, right?" he said, galloping down the steps.

"A minor." What the hell was up with Nico?

He waited for me at the bottom of the stairs. Then he beckoned me to follow. We hurried down a long corridor with no windows. At the end of it, he turned left into a small room.

The first thing that hit me was the odor. What was that awful smell?

Bertoni and Lou were sitting at a rickety wooden table. *Sitting* might not be the correct word. Bertoni had his head down on the table and appeared dead. Lou was slumped against the back wall.

An empty bottle sat on the table. Cases of similar bottles lined the right wall of the room.

"Hi, Gina," said Lou, opening an eye. "Wanna try some grappa?"

Holy shit! This must be bootlegging headquarters. What a good cover, in the bottom of the banquet hall. Who would ever think to check here?

"They're drunk," said Nico with disgust. "They were supposed to be looking after the still for Magda, and they're totally shit-faced."

"How long have they been like that?" I asked.

"No idea," said Nico. "But it doesn't look right in there."

"Wuz Gina doin' 'ere?" muttered Bertoni.

"She took chemistry in college. She might be able to help," explained Nico. He walked to the far door and threw it open.

I started to follow Nico into the room and stopped dead in the doorway.

A wall of vapor whooshed at me. The stinging kind that hurts your eyes and turns your throat raw.

"I don't know anything about stills, Gina. But this doesn't seem right. Should it be overflowing like that?"

I peered into the room.

I'd only seen stills before on TV and in movies. I had visions of a large copper kettle over an open flame. Connected to the kettle would be a coil of copper tubing from which a trickle of clear moonshine would run into a glass jug.

The one in front of me was a high-end version, made of polished stainless steel. But the purpose of the apparatus was unmistakable. All the right bits were there, down to the blue flame of the propane burner under the kettle.

It didn't take a chemistry degree to figure out something was very wrong. Alcohol was bubbling out of the top of the jug and spreading across the floor. Any minute now it would reach the propane flame.

"That's ethanol!" I said. "It's highly flammable. Nico, we've got to get everyone out of here right away."

"But—"

"You go upstairs right now and get Pinky and the girls out of the building. DO IT! NOW! Don't waste a second."

Nico knew me well enough to know I wasn't kidding. He turned and ran. I shut the door to the still room very carefully. Then I walked to the table and lifted the end of it with a jerk. Bertoni slid to the floor.

"Get up!" I yelled to them both. "We've got to get out of here. The still's going to blow."

"Wha'?" said Lou.

I kicked Lou in the leg. Then I kicked Bertoni even harder. I would have liked to kick him more, but there wasn't time.

"Get out of here right *now*. Take the nearest exit. I MEAN IT!"

I helped to haul them up. Then I shoved their miserable drunken bodies out the door.

There wasn't much more I could do. I had no idea how to stop the overflow.

I closed the door to the connecting room carefully and followed the boys into the hall.

Bertoni had made it to the end of the corridor. He pushed open a steel door and disappeared into daylight. Lou was right after him. I followed Lou but stopped just short of the door.

I scanned the walls for a fire alarm. There it was! I ran to it and pulled the bar hard.

The alarm was deafening. My heart was pounding like a jackhammer. Loud noises do that to me.

I hit the steel door, pushed hard and vaulted out into sunshine. Bertoni and Lou were standing a few feet away, looking dazed.

"Get over to the parking lot! As far away as you can," I ordered.

I didn't wait for them. I ran around the side of the building and up the laneway, to the front entrance.

Nico was standing by my car with Pinky and the old ladies. "Get farther back!" I waved my arms and yelled, "Down the driveway!"

Nico put his arm around Great-Aunt Rita and together they skedaddled. Pinky helped Mrs. Pesce, and Loose Trudy lived up to her rep. She was fast.

I took one look back at The Forum and hoped I wasn't right. Yes, it would be embarrassing, especially since I had pulled the fire alarm. But rather that than—

Boom!

"Holy shit!" yelled Bertoni, behind me.

Lou wet his pants.

THIRTEEN

Half an hour later, the fire trucks were still sloshing water into the back side of The Forum.

Pinky had taken the old ladies back to the retirement home. Loose Trudy wanted to stay and watch the "hotties"—firemen—but Mrs. Pesce won out in the end.

Lou and Bertoni were lying on the hillside up from the laneway, passed out. I stood beside them, feeling numb and sort of on guard. A lot of people would be wanting to kill those two for what they had done. Or, rather, hadn't done.

I was greedy. I wanted that pleasure for myself.

The afternoon was turning chilly. The air was acrid with smoke. I stood silently with my arms crossed over my chest, waiting for Nico to return. He had gone to speak to the fire chief or whoever was in charge.

I watched as Nico walked slowly up the laneway. He had both hands in his pockets. His black-rimmed eyes looked stunned.

"It blew out the back wall," said Nico. "Then the fire climbed to the second floor."

I stared at him blankly.

"The second floor, Gina," Nico said patiently. "The still was right under the ballroom."

Now I got it.

"The ballroom is going to be a mess," he said. "The windows blew out. They've got the fire mostly under control, but it's completely flooded in there. Not to mention the smoke. And I expect the floor is unstable or nonexistent. I can't imagine the damage."

Certainly not something you could fix in two days. That was for sure.

"I'm so sorry, Gina."

"I'm just glad we got everyone out okay," I said.

"Me too."

We stood beside each other in shared misery. I had lost my wedding hall. Nico had lost his beautiful decor. It was an altogether crap situation.

"Did you know a flock of crows is called a murder of crows?" Nico said, out of the blue.

Before I could kill him, my cell phone sang the *Godfather* theme. I glanced at Nico. "I don't think I can take any more bad news."

The caller was Sammy. "I have some bad news," he said.

I held my breath.

"Your wedding champagne has been stolen."

"Stolen," I repeated mechanically.

"New York is getting hammered by the ice storm, and the reception hall has burned down."

"I know about the hall," I said.

"Yeah, there might have been a still in the basement."

"Old news, Sammy. Anything more? 'Cause I really gotta go." I clicked off without waiting for his response.

All the airports would be closed in New York. My mom wasn't going to be here in time for the wedding.

Really, I was doing quite well. I wasn't even crying yet.

"I need to phone Pete now," I said, wondering how long I could stall the tears.

Nico nodded. "I'll just go see how the fire trucks are doing, shall I?"

I watched Nico slink down the laneway. Then I speed-dialed Pete. He answered immediately.

"The reception hall has burned down!" I said.

Pete started to laugh.

"It's not funny," I wailed. "Those blasted boys from Buffalo have blown up our wedding hall. I'm looking at it right now."

"How...?"

I didn't stop to explain. I was in full rant mode now, complete with swinging arms. "The wedding champagne has been stolen. My mom won't be here in time for the wedding. And now there won't be a reception. What are we going to *do*?"

Pete said, "I have an idea. Stay right where you are. I'll be there in ten."

* * *

He was there in ten.

I was sitting by myself on a low cement wall between two Roman columns, with my red coat wrapped tightly around me.

I was also enveloped in an odor of recently burned reception hall and bad moonshine.

I waited for Pete to come right up to me and lift me into his arms.

"You are sort of a mess," he said. I sniffled into his chest. "A cute mess," he said hastily, playing with my hair. "Except for... what *is* that smell?"

"Blown up grappa still."

I could feel the chortle start deep in his chest.

"It's not funny," I said, pushing back.

"It's sort of funny," said Pete. His whole body was shaking as he tried to control himself.

"Our reception hall just burned down!" I thudded a fist on his chest. "The wedding is in two days. What are we going to do?"

I stared at him, eyes wide. His face went from laughing to serious. Very serious.

"Elope," he said.

I froze.

"You're kidding." I searched his face to see if he was.

"I mean it. Come with me right now. We'll go back to the condo, pick up what we need and just go."

"And leave everyone in the lurch?" It was unthinkable. Aunt Pinky would kill me. Not to mention Aunt Miriam, Aunt Vera and—oh my god—Nico. Nico, who had worked for days and days on the black-and-pink decor, for the hall that no longer existed...

"Listen to me." Pete put both hands on my shoulders. He pushed me back to look right into my eyes. "Do you really love me?"

"Of course I—"

"Then let's do this. Right now. No more bad-luck omens, no stolen anything. We just get on a plane, fly away from this burg, away from the family. And get married."

He was pleading. I could see it in his eyes. And just like that, I knew it was the right thing to do.

"Okay," I said with a quick intake of breath. "But where? The airports east of here are all closed."

Now he grinned. "Vegas, baby."

"Vegas." I could feel my heart lifting. "That's a wonderful idea! Lainy is singing there right now. She can still be my maid of honor. Can I tell her?"

"Yes, you can tell her. But no one else. No family."

"Vegas!" I said, clapping my hands. "We're getting married in Vegas. Hey! I have a cousin in Vegas."

Pete sighed. "Of course you do."

ACKNOWLEDGMENTS

I want to thank all the usual suspects: Cathy Astolfo, Alison Bruce, Cheryl Freedman, Don Graves, Joan O'Callaghan and Nancy O'Neill. Your support of me and this series is something I treasure

Warm thanks also to my many friends at the Hamilton Literacy Council. You give me purpose, and a whole lot more.

Lastly, this couldn't happen without Ruth Linka and the whole team at Orca Books. They take my wacky tales and turn them into something magical. I am forever grateful.

DON'T MISS
Gina Gallo's
OTHER ADVENTURES!

"Campbell tells a hilarious story of the goddaughter of a mafia leader drafted into a jewel-smuggling operation."
— *Ellery Queen Mystery Magazine*

"Campbell's comic caper is just right for Janet Evanovich fans. Wacky family connections and snappy dialog make it impossible not to laugh."
— *Library Journal*

MELODIE CAMPBELL got her start writing stand-up comedy. Her fiction has been described by editors and reviewers as "wacky" and "laugh-out-loud funny." Winner of ten awards, including the 2014 Derringer and the 2014 Arthur Ellis for *The Goddaughter's Revenge*, Melodie has over two hundred publishing credits, including forty short stories and eleven novels. She is the former executive director of Crime Writers of Canada. She lives outside Toronto, Ontario. For more information, visit www.melodiecampbell.com.

2014 Arthur Ellis Award winner for Best Novella
2014 Derringer Award winner

"A novella with legs and laughter…Strong plot, great zingers and imagery that draws you in and just doesn't let go…The scam is delightful, the plot, setting and dialogue move with page turning intensity which makes the Artful Author's third crime ride a blast and a laugh."

— Don Graves

RAPID READS
WWW.RAPID-READS.COM